GW01271289

Zombie Survival Guide

The essential guide to surviving the zombie apocalypse in post-Brexit Britain.

By Benjamin Seabrook

Fourth Edition

June 2031

Reviews for the Third Edition

"I've read worse."
Margaret Shaw, North Sheffield Gazette

"Extracts a dazzling poetry from the usually dry field of international law. I simply can't wait for the inevitable musical adaptation."
Philip James, Journal of Household Products

"Dangerous in its inaccuracy. If you in any way rely on the contents of this book you'll be arrested, killed or worse"
Walter Hopkins, Horse and Hound and Zombie Magazine

"Indispensable."
Jayne Holcomb, Preston Public Library

"I've followed my lawyer's advice and burnt my copy. I suggest you do the same"
Aiden Finch, Cornish Border Patrol

Contents

details of changes to food safety

Frequently Asked Questions – kindly supplied by readers of previous editions of this guide and answered by an elite team of self-proclaimed experts.

Introduction

Post-Brexit Britain is surely one of the safest, most pleasant countries on the planet. Still, complacency leads to mistakes and mistakes lead to death from flesh eating zombies.

All citizens are encouraged to read this authoritative guide to **fully** understand:

- How Brexit changed Britain for the better and why is means we have a world leading 1.5% zombie infection-rate.

- Changes to UK arrangements for travel, health, security and employment including the recently signed ZombiEU Act.

- Adapting to our new society where we're living side-by-side with the Dead.

This fourth edition of the **Post-Brexit Zombie Survival Guide** has been updated with the latest legislation from the UK, EU and United Nations Zombie Organization (UNZO).

Corrections to the Third Edition

Owners of the third edition of this guide should make note of the following corrections. The author is grateful to those readers who reported these errors either directly or through their legal representative. Apologies are made for injuries, deaths and other inconveniences that occur due to errors in this edition and all previous editions. Owners of the first edition must dispose of the guide immediately for their own safety and the safety of others.

1. Page 53 mistakenly describes Gillingham, Kent as a designated safe haven. This should have read Gillingham, **Dorset**. Gillingham, Kent has been declared a grade 7 radiological exclusion area.

2. On page 72 the maximum running speed of a fresh zombie is incorrectly listed as 12km/h. This should read 21km/h. The associated FAQ entry *"Can I easily out-run a fresh zombie?"* has similarly been updated.

3. The build instructions on page 102 for the Rad-Spike Zombie Dispersal device uses the wrong units for Plutonium-238. It

obviously should read 5mg instead of 5kg. Apologies to the residents of Gillingham, Kent.

History

> *"Call it foresight, call it luck, call it leadership genius. We find ourselves uniquely placed to use the power of Brexit to withstand the upcoming Zombie Apocalypse."*

> *British Prime Minister, August 2017*

As we adjust to this fourth decade of the 21st century it is worth remembering how we got here and why the UK is flourishing while so much of the world is shivering in the shadow the of undead.

Perhaps you're reading this guide from the comfort of your own Zanderson shelter or perhaps you're reading this by electric light in the northern fortress of Manchester. Wherever you find yourself the UK has changed immeasurably in the last decade. Of course, we now know the story starts over a century ago far away from the natural wonders of Britain, in the darkest corners of the continent we still call Europe.

Timeline of Events

1918 – the *Spanish Flu* H1N1 influenza pandemic kills an estimated 50 million people worldwide. In the UK a quarter of the population are infected and 250,00 die. The spread of the disease in thought to rapidly increase in the UK when soldiers returned home from mainland Europe at the end of WW1.

1920 – samples of the H1N1 virus are secretly stored at the Clear Rock Institute, at that time known for anti-ageing remedies. The details are still unknown but it is thought that their research continued for the remainder of the 20th century.

June 2016 – the UK votes to leave the EU in a referendum. Street parties last for as long as 3 days in many parts of the country.

August 2016 – after just two months of negotiation the UK and EU rubber stamp the Withdrawal Agreement. The agreement is swiftly passed by the UK Parliament and the UK leaves the EU on August 31st 2016.

October 2016 – the Preliminary USA/UK Trade Deal is agreed. This wide-ranging deal controversially includes the import of chlorinated chicken from the USA into the UK.

February 2017 – 5 miles from a German Clear Rock site there are reports of unusual chicken behaviour at a poultry abattoir. From leaked accounts we now know this is the first confirmed case of reanimation from the mutated H1N1 virus (mH1N1). Over the next two months similar reports emerge from mainland Europe, Asia, Africa and South America. There are no reports of zombie chickens from North America, triggering accusations of a cover-up. Despite concerns in the EU over food safety the chicken is permitted to be used in food production. This is primarily due to no existing legal restrictions on meat from reanimated dead-stock.

June 2017 – first reports of human infection from consuming contaminated chicken. A UN study subsequently finds that all chicken not washed in chlorine contains the mH1N1 virus. All chlorine-washed chicken from the USA is declared safe to eat. In the UK infections rates are below 0.1% as by this stage 98% of all chicken consumed in the UK is imported from the USA.

August 2017 – Global Outbreak. Infected humans begin to mutate and spread the virus through *'dental-epidermal contact'*. The pandemic infects 25% of the global population. Enhanced UK border controls put in place since Brexit contribute to the incredibly low 1.5% infection rate.

December 2017 – UN Agreement on Zombie Control Measures. Financial aid and logistical support is provided to all areas with an infection rate above 5%.

April 2018 – The EU Treaty on Zombie Rights (aka ZombiEU) becomes law in all 27 EU member states. After widespread campaigns by the two main pro-Zombie groups (EuroZombie and The mH1N1 Survivors Alliance) zombies are granted the 3 Rights:
1. All zombies are entitled to a **Living Death**
2. All zombies have **freedom of movement** within the Schengen Plus Area.
3. All zombies can apply for **family unification** within EU member states and with those third-countries that countersign the treaty.

July 2018 – UK EU Zombie Agreement. In return for a basic trade agreement the UK adopts the EU Treaty on Zombie Rights (ZombiEU). The following month this is passed into UK law as the Minimal Zombie Rights Act 2018.

The World Today

Excerpt from the UN Joint Statement on Zombie Control (February 2018):

> *"Today the dead are subdued. A great tragedy has ended, not with victory, but with survival. A new era is upon us bringing with it profound concern, both for our future security and the survival of civilization. We are committed to the Matlock Declaration of principles that see that the Dead can express their freedom of expression, freedom of action and freedom of thought. We, the Living, are committed to defend these freedoms through the application of force, application of control and the instruments of power.*
>
> *Properly directed, the Dead can once again elevate themselves to a position of consequence and walk side-by-side with the Living in mutual respect and for mutual benefit. For the Living the benefits may be momentous."*

The Dead are under control. Under **our** control:

Designated Zombie Areas
In the UK and much of Europe the Dead live en masse in Designated Zombie Areas (DZA). In the UK there are 5 DZAs: Milton Keynes, Colchester, Truro, Glasgow and Aberystwyth. Within each DZA the Dead are free to roam and form their own societal norms. While there are some Living humans in each DZA for security and monitoring, there are no Living residents.

Domestic Zombie Permits
Zombies can reside with Living hosts in the home environment. This typically allows for families to remain together after one or more family members have started zombification. Citizens may also house non-family members through the government's Adopt-A-Zombie scheme.

Zombie Employment
The UK is the world leader in providing jobs for the Dead with a zombie unemployment rate of just 5% (based on June 2030 figures). Despite record employment levels for the Living there have been recent changes to the law to give priority to the Living over the Dead. Employers must advertise jobs first to Living applicants before allowing the Dead to apply.

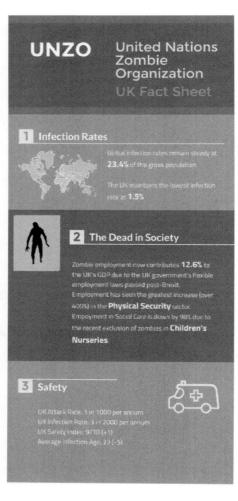

UNZO

United Nations Zombie Organization

UK Fact Sheet

1 Infection Rates

Global infection rates remain steady at **23.4%** of the gross population

The UK maintains the lowest infection rate at **1.5%**

2 The Dead in Society

Zombie employment now contributes **12.6%** to the UK's GDP due to the UK government's flexible employment laws passed post-Brexit. Employment has seen the greatest increase (over 400%) in the **Physical Security** sector. Employment in Social Care is down by 98% due to the recent exclusion of zombies in **Children's Nurseries**

3 Safety

UK Attack Rate: 1 in 1000 per annum
UK Infection Rate: 3 in 2000 per annum
UK Safety Index: 9/10 (+1)
Average Infection Age: 23 (-5)

UNZO

Latest UN Factsheet on UK Zombie Control

Travel

Some of the first, misguided, concerns from UK holidaymakers post-Brexit related to ease of travel within the EU, health insurance, visas and passport pigmentation. Now that the EU is literally crawling with the undead the plucky Brit Abroad must consider a multitude of bureaucratic matters from Schengen Plus to Quarantine Zones, from Border Security to Visa Applications. This section of the book will guide you through this metaphorical minefield and ensure you avoid the literal minefields of southern Italy.

Before travelling outside the safety of the UK you should first ask yourself *"Do I really need to go to Europe?"*, to help answer this the travel company McAllister South West Holidays helpfully provide the following tips:

1. Are you aware that during the zombie outbreak in August 2017 FCO advised against all travel to all EU member states?
2. Did you know that Weston-Super-Mare was voted the UK's most popular sea-side resort on no fewer than 3 occasions? (1963, 1964 and 1967).

3. Consular support in many EU states is still **severely** limited to emergency assistance, medical assistance, postal services, free wi-fi and children's day-care (excl. weekends and UK Bank Holidays).
4. Did you know that Weston-Super-Mare is rated as OFSTEZ Outstanding for zombie security? The A370 access road was recently rebuilt with 5-meter-high concrete defences!
5. Due to current export restrictions you will find Parisian cafés are struggling to meet demand for staples such as black pudding, kippers, haggis, laver-bread and jellied-eels. Come to a sea-side restaurant overlooking the clear blue waters of the Bristol Channel and you'll be enjoying a true culinary feast.

If you've got this far and are *still* considering a trip to Europe then read on.

Schengen Plus Area

The Schengen Area was established in 1995 and allowed all living Europeans to move between member states without passports and without encountering controls at the border.

Prior to the Global Outbreak of 2017 there were over a billion crossings a year between countries in the Schengen area. Of the pre-Brexit 28 EU states, 22 of them participated in the Schengen Area. The UK was opted out of the Area and maintained border controls.

With the ZombiEU treaty came the formation of the Schengen Plus Area (**SPA**). The Area is now larger and more complex, it includes Bulgaria, Croatia, Cyprus and Romania – all countries formally legally required to join. The UK maintains a partial opt-out whereby it is part of the SPA with additional maximum border security controls.

Under ZombiEU rules:
- All zombies are entitled to freedom of movement within the SPA.
- Zombies travelling in or out of the SPA can apply for a SPA Visa. There are several Visa types.

- Zombies must be microchipped, meeting standards ISO11784 and ISO11785. They must also have a valid ZombID card. You can get your zombie microchipped at your local vets.

Visas

A zombie visa can be applied for in any of the SPA countries and allows freedom of movement inside the entire SPA. There are several types of visa available with different restrictions that apply in accordance with the zombie's circumstances.

Family and Friends
Zombies who have family or friends in a Schengen Plus member state can travel on this visa. The visa application must be completed by a **living** family or friend.

Cultural and Sports
This visa applies to zombies travelling to Europe for attending Cultural events such as the *Deptford Dearly Departed Festival* and Sports events such as the *Margate Mortified Marathon*. Fox hunting is **not** considered a Sports Event for the purpose of a

SPA visa if zombies are being used in place of foxes or hounds.

Business
As you'll learn later there are countless job opportunities for hard working zombies in the UK. Indeed, death is no longer the obstacle to steady employment that it used to be. Zombies can travel on a SPA Business Visa of varying lengths from 3 months to 2 years depending on their current decomposition state as measured on the Marfleet Scale.

Airport Transit
The purpose of this Visa is for zombies who are travelling through the airport of a Schengen Plus country without entering the country. In the UK this is limited to Cardiff and Luton airports where the departure lounges include level 5 quarantine facilities.

Heathrow is expected to again accept zombie travellers in the next 18 months with a new state-of-the-art and **dedicated** zombie quarantine facility. The original shared pet quarantine, having recovered from the unfortunate incident last summer, has now been deep cleaned and is fully operational.

Health

Healthcare for the Living and the Dead is a strategic priority for the UK. It is of course true that the mH1N1 virus has put additional strain on the health services, not least because citizens are now making use of those services long after their death (a period when traditionally citizens would cease receiving medical care). Brexit meanwhile has delivered an invigorating freedom from regulations allowing the UK government to reshape all aspects of the health system.

European Medicines Agency (EMA)

The EMA is the EU agency responsible for evaluating and supervising medical products. Pharmaceutical companies submit new medicines to the EMA for testing and approval for use in the EU. Once approved by the EMA the medicines can be marketed and used in all EU, EEA and EFTA states.

As the UK officially left the EU it meant leaving the jurisdiction of the EMA. The benefits are clear: medicines within the UK are evaluated by a new sovereign agency (UKMA) by an experienced but lean workforce. The UKMA headquarters in Kilmarnock houses an elite team of two pharmaceutical experts who are able to process a new medicine through all stages of approval in a world beating three days. Regulators found this compared very favourably with the average of 144 days with the EMA and 170 days with the US FDA.

The UKMA is Scotland's largest zombie employer, a fact that goes some way to explain why it is based at the former site of the Dean Castle and Country Park. Working in relative safety while peering through the windows of the 14th century castle, UKMA living staff can monitor the 25,000 zombie employees wandering the 200 acres of green fields and woodland.

Our domestic medical-testing market was significantly reshaped and boosted by the UK's withdrawal from EU testing regulations (including EU Cosmetics Directive 76/768/EC). While the original law set out to prohibit testing on animals its removal has given UK agencies the freedom to test medicines, cosmetics and other microbiological agents on the Dead. Fresh zombies make especially good candidates for medical test subjects – they share the same DNA as humans and are physiologically 60% similar to the Living (on par with the humble goat).

Recent UKMA work at Dean Castle has included several new medicines safely and rapidly tested on the Dead:

- Macrobulin Adasol: a muscle stimulant tested on zombies housed in the Dean Castle Adventure Playground. Results indicated an unexpected asymmetrical effect on the test subject's muscles. Only the right-hand side of the body benefited from the stimulant effect causing all zombie employees to walk in counter-clockwise patterns. Macrobulin Adasol is approved in the UK for use in competitive track athletics.
- Pralistrel Rosidocin: an appetite reduction drug evaluated by zombies housed in the castle's petting zoo. Based on observed behaviour in this single test environment the drug is approved for generic use in humans. To be taken twice daily with water after eating (recommended meals are Guinea pig curry, hamster carbonara and chinchilla stew).
- Drospixolol: a blood anticoagulant designed to prevent blood clots and reduce change of heart attack. Unusually the drug had a **pro**-coagulant effect on the test subjects, hardening the blood to such a degree that within 3 minutes all blood in

the body was solidified. Remarkably none of the subjects experienced a heart attack before solidification, therefore this drug was swiftly approved for use in adults and children over 12.

- Zyporin Progine: an effective remedy to treat hair loss. During the three-day trial phase, the zombie test subjects exhibited significant hair growth on the scalp, face, torso and limbs. Side effects **may** include breathing difficulties, vertigo, flatulence, hallucinations, muscle tearing and disorientation. Nonetheless, due to staff absence and the lack of effective control subjects, the informally reported side effects have not been substantiated. Zyporin Progine is available over the counter from your local pharmacist.

Qualifications

The Mutual Recognition of Professional Qualifications Directive (MRPQ) is the European legal instrument that allowed people gaining a professional qualification in one EU state to have that qualification automatically recognised in another. Many professions were covered by MRPQ and in healthcare it applied to doctors, dentists, nurses, midwives and pharmacists.

The viral outbreak significantly affected the numbers of EU health professionals in the labour market. Healthcare workers were 3 times more likely to be exposed to the mH1N1 virus resulting in a 75% infection rate among this critical group. The result? It's nearly impossible to attract suitably qualified EU health workers to the UK. Therefore, since 2027 the UK has operated the Flexible MRPQ scheme – a forward thinking approach that encourages diversity in the healthcare sector by recognising a wider range of degrees as equivalent to the legacy medical qualifications.

If you have any of the degree qualifications listed below, a career at the frontline of health could be yours (third-class honours or above required):

Fashion Design: use your sewing skills on exciting new materials including human skin, internal organs and blood vessels. Current vacancies include "Senior Blanket-Stitch Surgeon", "Cranial Backstitch Assistant" and "Catwalk Physiotherapy Manager"

Psychology: hundreds of thousands of students studied for a degree in psychology only to find that further study to doctorate level is needed before they're allowed anywhere near patients. Join your local hospital as a triage receptionist and you can pretend that you're using your degree every day. New government targets aim to reduce the burden on the health service 'at the front gate'. As a Triage Receptionist it would be your responsibility to quickly evaluate incoming patients for their honesty, mental wellbeing, physical capability, class, social standing and subsequent eligibility to receive medical care.

Archaeology: you love digging up old things but, in the UK, all the good stuff has already been found. New historical artefacts are not expected to be buried for centuries, so what career options are there? Imagine working at your local morgue where exhumations are now a weekly occurrence. Mysterious sounds from graveyards across the country hint at the fresh new zombies waiting to join their families in the sunshine.

Healthcare Employment

For further information on healthcare jobs refer to the Employment section of this guide.

Trade

Trade deals are complicated affairs that take on average 18 months to agree followed by another 45 months, on average, to actually implement. It's no wonder then, that what takes 5 years on sunny days is taking decades against the backdrop of an apocalypse.

The post-Brexit trade aspirations of the government were thrown into disarray when the Dead began roaming the Earth. Priorities changed and goods & services once considered important now seemed irrelevant. The UK's number one export prior to 2018 were cars (approx. £25 billion per year) – whereas now there are three drivable cars per living adult and new cars are naturally not needed. The sole remaining British car manufacturer is LEVC who are responsible for electric London taxis. There is unfortunately a limited market for London cabs outside the UK mainland.

In a nutshell the UK trading position is now covered by three elements:
1. The comprehensive 2016 USA-UK trade deal signed immediately after the withdrawal agreement.

2. The basic EU trade deal signed as part of the UK's adherence to the ZombiEU legislation. Approximately 98% of this EU trade deal applies to the UK car industry and permitted continued use of just-in-time supply chains and tariff free trade between the two partners.
3. WTO rules cover all other trades. More on this commercial wonderland later.

The Strength of the Weak Pound

Let's begin with a positive – the Great British Pound is at the time of writing worth $0.32. Ever since the USA was invented in 1776 the pound has typically hovered around the $5 mark. For a brief period during the US Civil War the dollar saw massive depreciation and one pound would buy $10 – an especially good decade for British holiday-makers. Post-World War II however the pound has steadily lost value as the UK property market crashed (1980s), withdrawal from the ERM (1990s), Financial Crisis (2000s), Brexit (2010s) and Zombies (2020s) all took their toll.

Of those who are celebrating the weak pound it is perhaps firms exporting from the UK who are likely to be smiling widest. The combination of a historically low exchange rate with a reshaped society has given birth to some unusual success stories:

Home Exports: estimates put the number of abandoned UK homes at 3.5 million as families share homes with fortified defences and millions migrate to stronghold cities such as Manchester. It's now far cheaper for prospective US home owners to purchase an entire UK home and ship it across the Atlantic than it is to build from scratch in the USA. A 4-bed detached family home can be snapped up for an irresistibly low price of $3,500. Pending planning permission, the next stage in home exports is the controversial Swindon Project 2040 that aims to export the entire town (minus the contaminated Wyvern Theatre) from Wiltshire to Massachusetts. Wiltshire's loss is surely America's gain with Historic Swindon, MA likely to be a popular tourist destination.

History: announcing the Great British History Reduction Programme the Secretary of State for Culture explained: "*For two thousand years our great country has built layer upon layer of rich history – and let's not forget the splendour of other nations that our amazing Empire transported atop dangerous roaring oceans to the safety of our museums. I say to you today, this has to stop, we can no longer be the warehouse for the world's treasures with no show of gratitude or recognition of the service we've provided. Our children too, are overwhelmed by centuries of*

*kings, queens, wars, revolutions, discoveries and
conquests. There's frankly no need to learn about most
of this history when even the edited highlights are
enough for a full, rich and rewarding education. So
today I am proud to announce a two-pronged attack on
this monumental problem. Firstly, this government
will select the very best from our past to author the
Official British History (843-2030). Secondly, all
artefacts, literature and buildings that do not form
part of the official history will be auctioned for the
benefit of all citizens. All the funds from the auction,
the History Bonus as we call it, will provide the capital
investment needed to keep the UK safe. Stronger cities.
More weapons. Higher walls. Fewer zombies
wandering lost on our streets. More zombies working
for us. We will be Stronger Together."*

The History Reduction Programme was a great
success with the frail pound permitting other
countries to snap up a trove of veritable bargains.
Ultimately generating £1.5 trillion to invest in
construction projects such as the Triple Plus
border wall (see the Security section for more
details), so successful was the auction that the
official history is now fully optimised:

- Before the year 2000 the UK had one
  prime minister, Winston Churchill, who
  bravely led the UK from 1940 to 1955.
  Prior to WWII the monarch governed
  absolutely and it is assumed that

Parliament was prorogued from 1955 until the turn of the millennium.

- There have been just three British monarchs, the confusingly named King Henry VIII, Queen Victoria and Queen Elizabeth II. Due to the superior genetics of the upper classes the monarchs were particularly long lived. Henry VIII was 346 years old by the time of his death in 1837 and as every schoolchild knows he is most famous for his 28 wives.
- The existence of many UK landmarks fundamentally conflicted with the official history so they have been exported or repurposed. Commuters through Tokyo's Shinjuku district can now marvel at the iconic Stonehenge and wonder at how the sandstone found its way to Japan (it was, of course, carried by zombies). Meanwhile the Eden Project now houses the UK Tropical Zombie Training Complex where Special Forces practice combat techniques against the Dead for overseas missions. It also makes a fantastic venue for children's parties if all parents are willing to sign the extensive waiver.

WTO rules

Aside from the USA nearly all trade between the UK and other countries is under World Trade Organization (WTO) rules. The WTO sets the tariffs that must be paid when importing goods to a country – a tariff is a tax paid by the importer to the government of the importing country e.g. if you want to import bananas into the UK then under WTO rules you must pay the UK government £95 per 1000kg of bananas. For all the apprehension of moving to WTO rules this has turned out to be a magnificent tax goldmine for the government. What had previously been tax free trading with the EU now earns the UK government £45 billion annually, while WTO rates with other nations adds another £65 billion of income.

The WTO, like the UN, APPLE, NATO, and other international organisations has had to evolve to meet the challenges of the zombie apocalypse. For the WTO this means publishing a revised list of *non-preferential tariff rates and quotas* – that is the charges a government must make on imports unless a trade deal takes precedence. Where no trade agreement exists, you must comply with Most Favoured Nation (MFN) rates. The complete list of tariffs and quotas are available on the WTO website, but here's a sample to whet your appetite:

Aluminium foil: in rolls of weight <= 10kg.
    MFN tariff rate 7.5%

Bananas, fresh (excluding plantains).
    MFN tariff rate £95 per 1000kg

Anti-Viral Zombie Repellent: unit sizes <= 250ml
    MFN tariff rate 25%

Kevlar (including other aramid fibres) in sheets
up to 2.5mm thickness.
    MFN tariff rate £170 per 100kg

Fruit & nut chocolate bars, individually wrapped.
    MFN tariff rate 12.5%

Bioethanol, undenatured with alcoholic strength
of >= 80% for use as fuel
    MFN tariff rate 21%

Firearms inc. handguns, long guns, semi and
automatic.
        MFN tariff rate 75%
        (USA tariff rate 5%)

Vegemite Yeast Extract, unit sizes <= 2kg
    MFN tariff rate 30%

State Aid

If a business receives government financial support it benefits from an advantage over its competitors – this is State Aid. Members of the EU must comply with strict EU state aid rules that generally prohibit the government from saving businesses from failure which directly contributes to job losses, the breakdown of family life, homelessness and a 52% fall in measurable happiness.

In the past the UK government has been unable to provide state aid to important sovereign businesses. Take the example of British Steel that was threatened with insolvency when the government were unable to provide state aid. Why? The EU Commission believed that too much steel was produced in Europe and frowned upon state aid in this industry. The UK's steel output at the time was a mere 4% of the EU total – a figure that was dwarfed by the 26% produced in Germany. We can count ourselves lucky that following the UK's exit from the EU there was a rapid increase in demand from the zombie outbreak – steel walls, fences, knives, armoured vehicles all needing manufacturer by skilled, dedicated, hardworking British engineers. The £4.2 billion cash injection kept factories open, kept families united and most importantly for investors it contributed to a 1500% increase in the company's share price.

It's not just big business that can now benefit from government investment and part-ownership. The UK Small Zombie Business Aid Scheme (UKSZBAS) provides state aid for small enterprises who are directly contributing to the UK's status as *The Safest Place on the Planet*.

- **Loans & Grants** of up to £500K are available to charities and other non-profit making bodies (including UK Manufacturing) that provide zombie security goods and services.
- **Tax breaks**, including enhanced capital allowances can be granted to UK companies whose workforce is 5% zombie employee or higher.
- **State assets** may be used for free or at less than market price for businesses providing zombie imprisonment and habitation services. It is through this very scheme that Windsor Castle is now home to the *Zombie Health, Mindfulness and Incarceration Spa* with world class rehabilitation rooms for zombies in need.

All good citizens should mark their diaries and remember that every September since 2025 the

State-Aid charity event has been raising money from the always generous UK public to directly fund government state aid projects. Ever since the smash hit single *"Do the Dead Know It's Christmas?"* kick-started the first State-Aid event it has raised a colossal £125 billion from public donations. That's £125 billion that would otherwise have had to be raised through higher corporation tax, closing government golf courses or re-applying VAT to luxury products.

Weapons
Our final topic on Trade considers that most important aspect of everyday life – adequate and effective defence against the Dead. If you're planning to import weapons for home defence, personal protection or team building events, it's important to understand the rules and regulations that govern imports to the UK. For the most part these rules and regulations are a direct result of the UN Arms Trade Treaty (ATT). The ATT is a multilateral treaty, signed in 2014, that regulates the international trade in conventional weapons. The UK ratified the ATT in 2014 and remains a signatory, still some significant amendments were introduced in 2024 allowing the import of weapons for zombiecide – these imports must be declared as *"destined for use in zombie control and extermination where risk to*

Living individuals is minimised through acoustic announcements and appropriate signage".

Additionally, it is worth noting that the UK is no longer bound by the EU ban on the import of torture equipment (regulation EC 2019/125) and many useful bits of equipment can now be brought into the UK legally for controlling the Dead. Recommended equipment includes, but is not limited to, electric chairs, drug injection systems, restraints, shackle boards, cage beds, batons & truncheons with metal spikes and barbed whips.

Security

Leading up to the 2015 general election the most important issues to voters were the Economy, Health and Immigration. Fast-forward nearly a decade and prior to the 2024 election the British public were most anxious about one thing – Security. It's no surprise then that the UK Security Party secured 63 parliamentary seats and has proved a challenging coalition partner for the government.

Let's begin with the quintessential symbol of any country's security – the border.

UK Border

After Brexit the UK was keen to *finally* take control of its borders. Government ministers were disappointed to find, on closer examination, that the UK already enjoyed full control of its own borders. Unlike other EU member states the UK was not part of the Schengen passport-free area, meaning it retained border controls.

Undeterred, the UK embarked on a public consultation exercise to architect a British border everyone could support. This consultation, arbitrated by the free press, designed a full range of new sovereign border controls. Dubbed "UK Border Plus Plus", this new 21st century border saw many new improvements:

1. A new Ultra-Fast Entry lane for exclusive use by UK citizens. The 300 UFE lanes at Heathrow airport permit UK citizens entering the UK to literally sprint from their aircraft to the airport exit in just 3 mins. The famous Portsmouth UFE Waterslide is a particularly fun and refreshing way to enter the country.
2. A Right-Stuff Questionnaire to be completed by all non-UK nationals entering the UK. The questionnaire ensures all those entering the country exhibit desirable characteristics. Questions cover essentials such as queueing stamina, tea (milk first), scones (jam first), apologising and imperial units.
3. A complimentary handshake and knowing wink for all **blue** passport holders crossing the border.

UK Border Plus Plus was an instant success with the Daily Mule (a Border Platinum Sponsor), declaring it "*the most beautiful, strong, perfect border in the world*". While clearly a strong & perfect border it was not ultimately zombie proof leading to a revised, more perfect border being built under the UK Border Plus Plus Plus scheme.

The final Triple Plus border guarantees that the UK is zombie proof in several ways:

1. The full 7,723 miles of UK coastline are now protected by the 33ft high zombie-proof Gerevich Fence. Retrofit installation of gates (requested by countless coastal communities), is now progressing in earnest.
2. A new Zombie Entry lane is in operation at all UK ports. Often mislabelled as "quarantine" these humane 100-mile lanes allow zombies to shuffle into the UK within 2-3 months of seeking entry.
3. Installation of 650 Armada Watchtowers placed every 12 miles along the border at a cost of £32 billion. Despite funds for staffing the Armada system never arriving, the very presence of the imposing steel and concrete watchtowers is enough to give any zombie second thoughts about entering the UK illegally.

Border Operations

Establishing the big beautiful border, while a significant and much adored step, was still but a single step in our marathon to secure Britain.

Before we'd even broken into a sweat the government turned its bureaucracy-reducing gaze towards Border Operations. While this might sound like a fantastically exciting world of high-stakes, cat and mouse games between nefarious smugglers and our intrepid border force, it is in fact an incredibly dull world of form filling, red tape and economy-wrecking time wasting. Well, no longer! The new UK border is a place of ruthless efficiency, minimal oversight and startling incidents every day.

Recent recruit James Kettler recently moved from Army bomb disposal to border force vehicle inspector: *"It's the anticipation I enjoy the most I suppose. The vehicles arrive with no paperwork you see, we don't know where it's from, it could contain anything. Just this morning my hand was hovering over a truck's rear door handles, my mind racing with what I was going to find – zombies? Wild animals? Explosives? Not today, no sir. That was just an illegal shipment of fruit & nut chocolate bars. That's the problem with confectionary you see, very quiet, hard to detect."*

Dangerous Goods
The movement of dangerous goods is regulated by the "European Agreement concerning the International Carriage of Dangerous Goods by Road" (ADR). During the Brexit transition the

government of the day decided to retain the UK's obligations without change (lacking the foresight of the undead future that awaited us). These obligations, almost without consideration, were included in the ZombiEU legislation and so British transport companies must still abide by this EU treaty.

The dangerous goods laws cover a wide variety of materials that might not immediately sound especially dangerous – flammable gases, flammable liquid, flammable solids, infectious substances and radioactive material. All of which could be transported more quickly and more cost effectively if it wasn't for the noose of EU red tape.

Picture the scene, one rainy Thursday afternoon in a Kensington vegan cafe, so the story goes, the Secretary of State for Transport was reading through her favourite acts of parliament when she happened upon a remarkable detail in the dangerous goods legislation: *"… if you transport dangerous goods by air, sea, road, rail or inland waterway, you must abide by these regulations."* The Secretary of State for Transport quickly finished her falafel wrap, grabbed her umbrella and sprinted to the nearest international trade lawyer. Fortunately, in Kensington this was not a long sprint.

Air, Sea, Road, Rail or Inland Waterway are the only transport mechanisms to which the dangerous goods legislation applies. **Any other** type of transport is exempt. Coupled with the Dead's appreciation for perilous tasks it wasn't long before the government shrewdly sidestepped a significant amount of red tape. UK companies now have several alternative shipment options:

1. The EuroCannon: Above the English Channel controlled air space begins at 500ft so anything under that altitude is, legally speaking, not travelling by air. The EuroCannon completed construction in 2028 and is capable of firing fully laden zombies from Calais to Dover at a velocity of 340 mph without ever exceeding an altitude of 300ft.

2. Foot – here's an amazing fact for you: The Dead can shuffle along carrying up to 6 times their own bodyweight making them excellent, environmentally friendly couriers. Delivery times can be disappointing so Foot transport is not recommended for perishables such as poppadoms or anti-viral medication.

3. Space: it's *really* high up. EU Law uses the Kármán line to define where airspace ends and outer space begins. The Kármán line is

drawn at 62 miles above sea level. Luckily the international community is not in complete agreement, the USA for instance draws the line at 50 miles. Free from the clamps of EU law the UK has since 2025 defined outer space as starting at an altitude of just 1 mile. There's now a fleet of UKCannons around the country firing goods-carrying zombies from one town to another. It has also inadvertently given a massive boost to the UK's bourgeoning space tourism industry with owners of light aircraft able to offer trips to outer space.

CITES Controls

The Convention on International Trade in Endangered Species of Wild Fauna and Flora (CITES) controls the trade in endangered or protected animal or plant species. With the UK now outside the EU all imports and exports with the EU now fall under CITES and European Council Regulation 338/97. This is a highly complex area of international law and readers should consult their own team of lawyers before initiating trading. With that caveat here's a couple of example scenarios to help you understand current industry practice:

1. **Hippopotami**: as one of the larger mammals on the controlled species list the

hippopotamus presents a unique challenge for shipping and delivery companies. Transport by zombie never got past the initial trials as zombies proved unable to work in the large teams needed to lift even a single hippo. We can at least enjoy the unusual sight of the Lake District's wild hippo herds. For now, hippos must be transported by the traditional sea, road and rail routes, until construction of the EuroCannon Extra Plus project is complete and shipments of up to 3 metric tonnes (2 hippos) can be swiftly sent between the UK and the continent.

2. **Zombies**: although it sounds counterintuitive, zombies are classed as an endangered species in the UK due to their low 1.5% proportion of the population. In the EU of course the common zombie or *morts commun*, makes up 25% of the population and does not fall under CITES control. In addition to a valid zombie visa, if you are importing a zombie to the UK from the EU or Rest of World you must apply for a permit by completing form **FED0172** (available online). When completing the form please use the scientific name of *Periculo Mortuis* rather than the zombie's given name e.g. Colin or David. It is highly recommended to use

the Post Office's "Zombie-Check" service for visa application forms.

Nuclear Deterrent

The UK has been a nuclear power since 1940 when research began under the secret Tube Alloys programme, leading up to the UK's first nuclear weapon test in 1952. The current deterrent consists of 120 warheads deployable from four Vanguard-class submarines armed with Trident missiles.

In Scotland especially, one of the key arguments during Brexit was on the issue of Trident and whether to scrap it or invest in the future of the UK nuclear deterrent. A political decision was neatly avoided when the zombie apocalypse collided with naval catering. While all on-shore catering supplies were sourced from the UK or USA, the navy continued to buy food from several EU suppliers. We still await an official report on the incident but leaked documents show that the Vanguard submarines took on-board significant supplies of Chicken Tikka Masala infected with the mH1N1 virus. On 15th November 2018, just one day after the ever-popular Wednesday Quiz and Curry night, all four submarines went unexpectedly radio silent. An off the record remark by a cabinet minister in 2019 revealed the seriousness of the situation: *"those four submarines, I mean, where the fuck are they? It's been months."* Now, over a decade later, there remains a good chance that there are nuclear armed zombies travelling the globe. We can of course take some comfort knowing that they are British zombies, travelling in British built vessels.

So, the UK finds itself in the politically pleasing situation that people on both sides of the Trident debate are happy. We simultaneously both have and do not have a nuclear deterrent. The official government line is that the UK remains a nuclear power, giving the current status as "Heisenberg".

Zombie Tracking

We all want to know where the Dead are 24 hours a day, 7 days a week. With that in mind, all zombies in the EU must be registered in their member state, implanted with a GPS-enabled microchip and carry their ZombID card at all times.

Within the EU all zombies are tracked and monitored at all times through their GPS microchip. Since 2026 GPS tracking has been provided by Europe's new Galileo GPS system. The post-Brexit wrinkle in this relates to the UK's decision in 2018 to cease involvement in Galileo and instead build a sovereign UK Global Navigation Satellite System.

Led by the UK Space Agency (UKSA) with a *"money is no object"* promise the new system is progressing well. Over 50 companies are collaborating from over 530 premises throughout the UK. Employing over 1 million skilled workers, the GPS system alone accounts for a full 6% of the UK workforce. Former car makers, nurses and police officers have found themselves re-skilling in security, cryptography and satellite manufacture. As the adverts say, it's easy to locate a job in GPS.

With the new GPS system scheduled to go operational in the 2070s the UK will continue to operate the innovative **Crowd Sourced Zombie Tracking** (CROSZT) system for the next four decades at a minimum. CROSZT is the world's most cost-effective zombie tracking system, built with British ingenuity and Blitz spirit. This remarkable solution is capable of tracking 30% to 40% of the UK zombies with an accuracy of 10km – repeatedly proven to be better than guesswork alone.

If you've not joined the CROSZT (pronounced "crossed") community then why not join today? Simply download the app to your smart device and you can play your part with the other 5 million CROSZT members, in keeping the UK safe and secure. Once armed with the CROSZT app simply scan the QR code on the ZombID card of every zombie you meet on your day to day business. You will of course meet zombies who do not prominently display their ZombID card. In those cases, just follow the app's instructions for Ask, Restrain, Scan and Run. Remember that for every QR code scanned the UK government contributes 0.01p to the CROSZT Members Memorial Fund – so get scanning!

Home security

The right to defend your home is now more important than at any time in Britain's history. Serious risks to your residence are so multitudinous that action must be taken. Wild nocturnal zombies may force their way into your home and attack while you sleep. Scavenging humans from the wrong side of town could lay in wait for you to open your doors and windows. Overseas visitors may become confused, angry and murderous while trying to understand simple British customs.

Fortunately for the concerned home owner, this is an area of UK life that has changed unquestionably for the better. We have the right to bear arms. Our personal obligations under the Human Rights Act have been significantly relaxed and the cost of quality weapons is now within the reach of ordinary workers thanks to a damn near-perfect trade deal with the USA.

Under UK Law:

- Anyone can use "reasonable" force to protect their home from intruders. Given that the Dead can often be up to 10 times stronger than their former breathing self, the courts have been generous on their acceptance of "reasonable". Those interested in case law should refer to *Connelly vs Wilson, Wilson, Wilson & Wilson (2027)*, in which abattoir worker Martin Connelly was found not guilty of murdering a family of four zombies who had the misfortune of walking into a garden defended by a trio of commercial cattle shredding machines.
- Victims do not have to wait until they are attacked before using force. Owners of scoped weapons would do well to remember this – if you feel in immediate

peril you can legally headshot a zombie up to 300ft away.

The range of home defence options are so diverse that a full list is beyond the scope of this book, so instead we'll focus on the most important and let's face it, the most fun options available to you. For a thorough understanding readers should pick up a recent edition of Shaefer's Home Improvement and Perimeter Security Encyclopaedia.

Traps
Since 1991, EU law (Council Regulation EEC No 3254/91) prohibited the use of leghold traps that were typically used to trap animals such as foxes and wolves. Over the last decade as the black market in imported traps from North America rose, several campaign groups pressured the UK government to act. The pro-trap *Zombie Conservation Association* wrote on their website *"Our professional zombie conservation community view trapping as an essential zombie management tool. Wildlife biologists have long recognised the role of trapping in control of density-dependent wildlife diseases such as mH1N1. Home owners are best placed to lead this conservation effort."*

Following the UK Domestic Protection Act 2029 it is legal for home owners to set leghold traps within the border of their property for protection from the Dead. To minimise risk of injury to living humans, appropriate signage must be displayed within 20ft of any trap. The Health and Safety Executive states that all signs must be at least 8 x 6 inches in size with clear text in a 12pt font reading "Keep off the Traps".

If anyone living triggers a home owner's trap, whether intentionally or not, they are liable under the Criminal Damage Act 1971 to financially compensate the home owner for any damage to the trap itself and any damage caused by zombies who would otherwise have been caught in the now occupied trap.

Approved trap types include Padded, Offset and Laminated although updated government guidance recommends **against** using offset traps. While offset traps are initially effective, they restrict blood flow and cause numbness in the trapped limb – this has often led to the Dead chewing off their limb and progressing further into the property.

Firearms

What better way to defend yourself, your family, friends, neighbours and passers-by than with your newly imported Muger Zr-556 automatic rifle? For those of us born before the 2020s this is a new and liberated country we find ourselves in, one where we're free to comprehensively arm ourselves for the safety of all.

This newfound freedom resulted from the UK's complete withdrawal from the European Firearms Directive and introduction of the UK Defence Emancipation Act (DEA) 2023. The DEA allows the general public to acquire weapons formally classed as Category A Prohibited firearms including explosive missiles, automatic firearms and ammunition with penetrating, explosive or incendiary projectiles.

With such vast defensive opportunities, it can be daunting for consumers to know what weapons they should invest in. The short guide below helpfully provides suggestions for the typical, day-to-day, life threatening scenarios home owners may find themselves in. While the author would like to think that the security of you and your family is of paramount importance (and therefore money-no-object), it seems sadly true that some consumers either choose to spend their money elsewhere or flatly refuse to work more hours. You'll find each scenario is accompanied by a Recommended option for the majority of buyers accompanied by, regrettably, a Budget option.

Essential Everyday Defence

The UK is a comparatively safe place to live when held up against the dangerous, violent, zombie-ridden landscapes of Columbia, Libya or Belgium. It doesn't pay to be complacent however, so citizens **must** consider how to defend themselves whilst going about their day-to-day business. Options here must be lightweight, affordable and able to provide a quick defensive response in hazardous situations.

- Recommended: Semi-Automatic Pistol. The ubiquitous *Evans & Thomas Model 25* pistol is produced in Bangor using the finest materials sourced exclusively from the UK. This easily concealed weapon is the ideal choice to fend of surprise attacks from the Dead, to threaten unsavoury Living humans or to forcefully make your way to the front of a ration queue.

- Budget Option: Chickpeas. Start making a dent in your Brexit stockpile of canned chickpeas by repurposing them for personal defence. By wearing the stylish *Evans & Thomas Chickpea Belt* you can carry from eight (28-inch waist) to fourteen (44-inch waist) cans of chickpeas. The belt's patented quick-release system will have you throwing rapid-fire chickpea cans at countless* advancing zombies.

up to fourteen, depending on defender's waist size.

Home Intrusion Defence

It's been said for hundreds of years: "An Englishman's home is his castle". Never has that been truer than in post-apocalyptic Britain. It stands to reason that any self-respecting patriotic home-owner will want to install several thousand pounds worth of British-made home-defence equipment. Options are diverse but this guide recommends the quality systems from Evans & Thomas (coincidentally a large corporate sponsor of this guide). All E&T systems come with a 2-month parts and labour warranty making all your purchases worry-free.

- Recommended: Automated Sentry Gun. The comfortingly expensive *Evans & Thomas 473-C Sentry Gun* is a tripod-mounted automatic machine gun designed to monitor and defend the perimeter of your home. While you and your family are sound asleep the 473-C will continuously scan for movement and partake in lethal action on your behalf. For the ultimate in home-defence you may upgrade to the 473-C *Pro Deluxe Sentry Gun* featuring advanced A.I. that not only detects movement but will intelligently spare the lives of passing cats, postmen, family and friends. Owners of the non-Deluxe model should simply remember to disarm the system as needed.

- Budget Option: Chickpeas. It may not look like much but the ordinary dried chickpea is five times stronger than a glass marble. As myriad 80s & 90s family movies demonstrated, a floor littered with dried chickpeas is an unpassable hazard of unrivalled magnitude. To fully protect a standard semi-detached home just scatter at least 30kg of dried chickpeas throughout the ground floor before bedtime (The *E&T ScatterMaster* makes light work of this). Come morning you'll discover any recent burglars or invading zombies incapacitated in a strictly horizontal position.

Home Defence at Range

Why wait until your home is under direct and

imminent threat? A typical cul-de-sac offers visibility of potential intruders at a range up to 400 yards. Residents of the Home Counties (even those with relatively modest estates) often enjoy a visible range of several miles. It is of vital importance that citizens install an effective medium to long-range defence system for their property.

- Recommended: Sniper Rifle. Since its introduction to the domestic market in 2028 the *Evans & Thomas K72B4 .50 Cal Sniper Rifle* has earned over sixty best-buy awards and is the long-range weapon of choice for the discerning marksman. The single-shot, bolt action gun comes with an effective range of up to 1.5 miles and can work with a suppressor to minimize muzzle flash and sound (ideal for pet owners). Parents will be encouraged to learn that thanks to the Evans & Thomas schools engagement programme it is likely that children of the household are already certified to operate the K72B4 rifle.

- Budget Option: Chickpeas. In creating the *E&T Chickpea Catapult* the company design team had a particular goal in mind, as E&T co-founder Fred Evans explains: *"we wanted to achieve the same lethal impact, the same momentum, with a can of chickpeas as we achieve with our popular K72B4 sniper rifle. The chickpea cans provide us with a fourfold increase in projectile mass compared with the .50 Cal ammo used in the rifle which translates into a target velocity of only 600 miles per hour."* And so, the Chickpea Catapult Mark One came to market in 2029 selling in most popular supermarkets and discount stores. The Mark Two is expected to be revealed early next year with a rumoured double-barrel and supersonic velocity.

Hordes

Finally, we come to the scenario that while unlikely in the UK we must still plan for – Hordes of zombies. Many of the defence systems discussed so far remain ineffective or worryingly short-lived against 100s or 1000s of the Dead. How would **you** defend your family when you open the curtains on a Sunday morning only to be presented with a sea of hungry, unhinged, zombie faces? The answer is with this guide's recommended option:

- Recommended: *The Evans & Thomas Rad-Spike Zombie Dispersal Device* is a commercially produced alternative to the dangerous homemade Rad-Spike devices that remained popular until a few years ago. Containing a short-range but lethal 5mg dose of Plutonium-238, the E&T Rad-Spike is delivered into the centre of an advancing horde whereby it detonates and eliminates all zombies within a half-mile radius. Each Rad-Spike comes with a complimentary pack of 50 anti-radiation suppositories for any Living humans caught within range (to be taken twelve hours **before** delivering the Rad-Spike device).

- Budget Option: Chickpeas. Radiation is again the preferred defence against hordes of zombies. Years of laboratory tests and first-hand accounts report that the Dead, particularly those from the south of England, are avid consumers of chickpeas. The common chickpea is unlikely to stop a zombie, but a **radioactive** chickpea – that's another story. For decades, overly cautious EU fire safety regulations mandated that homes should be fitted with expensive and unsightly smoke alarms. While you probably removed the batteries long ago, take a closer look inside your old smoke alarms and you'll find a radioactive chamber with a small amount of americium-241. Adding this radioactive material to a can of chickpeas for 48-72 hours will generate 250g (drained weight) of lethal chickpeas. A liberal sprinkling of radioactive chickpeas into a zombie crowd will quickly (approx. 7-10 days) result in elimination of the threat.

Employment

The UK is one of only 3 countries in the world (in addition to Aruba and Greenland) that allows the Dead to join the workforce.

Free from the shackles of EU Employment Law the UK ran a pilot scheme for zombie employment in 2020. The 'Cardiff Trial' as it become known was so successful that is was rolled out to the rest of the UK just 6 months later.

Employment Law Changes

There are a number of rights that did **not** stem from the UK's membership of the EU, including rights related to unfair dismissal, minimum wage, statutory redundancy pay and industrial action. These are largely retained for all employees.

The provisions in the ZombiEU treaty allow the UK to diverge from all rights stemming from EU Law for the **Dead** only.

So what rights are derived from EU Law and

how has the UK made zombie law fit-for-purpose, smart and forward looking for a Global Britain?

1. **Working Time** – EU Law demands that most workers are limited to a short 48-hour working week. This represents just 29% of the 168 hours available in every week! The Dead do not sleep. UK law permits zombie employees to work the full 168 hours (or 167 hours for unionised workforces).

2. **Holidays and Sick Leave** – UK law already exceeds the EU minimum (4 weeks) of holiday per annum and the Dead retain this right primarily for the benefit of Living family members to spend time with their loved ones. However, many rights on sick pay are derived from EU Law and is here that UK lawmakers have been particularly pragmatic in developing the rights for the Dead.

   a. During the **final** infection stage, post-mortem but pre-zombie, the employee is entitled to statutory sick pay for a period of up to 3 weeks. This excludes agency workers.

   b. 10 working days are permitted for recovery from loss of limb(s) if it is the result of an accident in the workplace. On return to work the employee may be offered a different role more suited to their new body shape. This right naturally **excludes** employees working in the sector formally known as Fox Hunting.

c. UK Law recognises that zombies at different stages on the Marfleet Decomposition Scale can endure varying levels of physical activity before irreversible body-mass loss occurs. Employees over Marfleet-5 can reduce to 150-hours per week and by an additional 10 hours for each additional Marfleet point.

3. **Redundancy Consultation** – this EU based right ensured that employers making 20-plus employees redundant are required to consult with an employee representative. New UK laws for the Dead have raised this trigger point to 1000 employees. In practice this affects only those employers making use of large zombie Hordes in their workforce.

a. A good example of this in practice is *'ZUnion North vs Great Mercia Trains (2021)'* – when GMT failed to consult when making over 3000 of their train-pulling employees

redundant.
4. **Data Protection (GDPR)** – the EU General Data Protection Regulation (GDPR) protects the personal information of individuals. Even under the ZombiEU treaty the Dead are considered 'data subjects' so UK companies still have obligations to their Dead employees. Changes for zombie data subjects include:
    a. Article 7: Conditions for Consent – a zombie must give consent to the processing of his or her personal data. Consent is assumed if when asked *"Do you consent to your personal data being processed?"*, the zombie doesn't verbally **decline** using clear and understandable language. Grunts, gurgles, roars, clicks, screams, moans and other non-verbal vocalizations are to be ignored. Welsh translators must be also be present for the avoidance of doubt.
    b. Article 17: Right to be forgotten - the data subject has the right for all data concerning him or her to be erased. Zombies simply have to personally complete forms ZEU-432, ZEU-435a and, if roaming in Scotland form ZEU-435b. Once

countersigned the form must be hand delivered to the Isle of Wight Zombie Administration Office, Newport. All forms must be completed in **black** ink and free from blood splatter, cranial mucus and gunshot residue.

c. Article 101: Extended Data Categories – the GDPR Article 9 (1) prohibits processing of personal data revealing race, ethnicity, beliefs, genetic and biometric data. Article 101 removes this restriction once the data subject transitions to their lifeless state. Article 101 (5) further extends the rights of data owners to store and process data relating to (a) the subjects current and historical Z-Tracker GPS location, (b) all incidents involving the data subject and suspected attacks on the Living, (c) the data subject's Marfleet decomposition stage and (d) any and all other types of data.

The Post-Brexit Jobs Market

Since the Brexit referendum the UK became a less attractive place to work for EU nationals, partly due to other parts of the EU recovering economically and the weakening Pound vs the Euro. The zombie apocalypse has only increased this pressure with improved visa controls and the emerging zombie employment market, cheerfully referred to as *Dead End Jobs*.

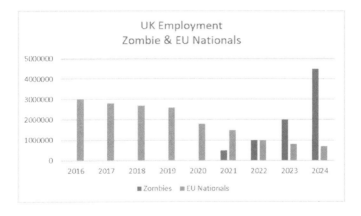

Of the industries impacted by the fall in EU workers the most significant pressure was seen in the four key sectors of Construction, Food, Healthcare and Childcare. In this chapter we will see how UK employment law has evolved to exploit the rising numbers of working Dead to not just fill the gaps left by EU workers but in many cases grow these critical industries.

Construction

The construction industry has seen perhaps the greatest growth from the zombie workforce. Industry leaders were initially sceptical with the head of the UCATT union saying in 2021 "*I fail to see how an employee exhibiting unpredictable movements, failing eyesight, a propensity to eat their colleagues and the mental capacity of a hamster is able to carry out a single one of the highly skilled jobs performed by our members*". Despite these concerns, zombies have since shown an aptitude for many construction jobs such as Masonry Worker, Roofer, Carpenter and Dry Wall Finisher.

The UK government, free from EU regulations, has supercharged the construction industry with two important policies – a massive reduction in Health and Safety bureaucracy for Dead employees and a world-leading apprentice scheme to ease zombies into the workplace.

Health and Safety Improvements

1. **Personal Protective Equipment (PPE) –** most obviously the construction industry

must meet their obligations imposed by EU directive 89/656/EEC i.e. employees are provided with hard hats, respirators, ear protection and other types of PPE. Exemptions are now enacted in the UK for zombie employees so that **no PPE** is required for the Dead workforce. Since 2024 this has saved the construction industry an estimated £120 million annually in equipment costs, allowing for a long overdue increase in senior management salaries. Employers are however still encouraged to follow the *Cranford-Smyth* cost benefit analysis method to determine the right level of PPE investment for their zombie employees. The classic case study, often quoted, is the Fylde Propeller Factory that used *Cranford-Smyth* in their decision to invest in protective clothing for their zombie workers – a simple change that reduced Dead staff turnover by 80% and factory cleaning costs by £50k per month.

2. **Mutagens, Ionising Radiation and Biological Agents (MIRBA)** – regarding the UK withdrawal from EU Directives 2004/37/EC, 2013/59/Euratom and 2000/54/EC. The UK Dead can now be freely exposed to many substances previously considered dangerous.

a. UK employers are no longer obliged to avoid exposing zombie employees to materials that would otherwise cause deep tissue burns, modify their DNA or present health problems such as death.
b. Industry has welcomed the MIRBA legislation and responded with business innovations including the *Single Use Employee*.
c. Single Use Employees are incredibly popular in the growing sectors of weapons research, hazardous waste disposal and in the clean-up of nuclear accidents – a service in which the UK is now a net exporter. We can barely keep up with demand!

Zombie Construction Apprenticeship Scheme

All zombie apprenticeship schemes are administered by ZUCAS with over 15,000 employers currently offering apprentice positions for the Dead. An estimated 45% of all apprentice placements are in the construction industry.

Common features of all schemes are:
- Potential recruits must show they have the ability to complete the programme.

Zombies must be at 3 or lower on the Marfleet scale. This provides assurance to employers that graduates from the scheme remain fit-for-work for at least 24 months.

- All apprentices receive the National Zombie Wage (fixed at 2% of the National Living Wage).
- Apprentices gain a range of transferable skills including obeying orders, coping with stimulus deprivation and operating in hostile environments.
- Graduates from a ZUCAS scheme gain a qualification of **Intermediate Level Apprenticeship** – generally considered to be the same as five GCSE passes or twelve Art degrees.

Food Industry

Following the vote to leave the EU the food and drink industry conducted a survey on their members and found that EU nationals accounted for on average 30% of the workforce and was particularly represented in Production Management, Quality Control and Logistics.

Post-Brexit changes to UK food laws have revitalised the industry and, with sensible regulations from the government, have allowed the UK to switch from a largely industrialised, polluting approach to a zombie-powered, green revolution.

EU regulation 178/2002 imposed many obligations on food businesses related to food safety, traceability of ingredients and the requirement to withdraw, recall or notify food when it is suspected of being unfit for human consumption.

Modern UK food law (The Food Safety and Hygiene Regulations 2026) is now fit-for-purpose:
- All ingredients from the UK are automatically considered Sovereign Quality. No traceability is needed.
- Food only needs to be withdrawn if it has

been proved, beyond doubt, in a UK court to be unsafe for human consumption. Food simply *suspected* of causing illness, or admittance to a morgue, need not be withdrawn from sale.

- Zombie Contamination (ZC) is acceptable in food products if it's measured to be at a safe level (at time of writing, ZC up to 17.5%). This generous ZC level allows employers to utilize the Dead in all parts of food production while UK consumers enjoy some of the lowest food prices in the world.
- Foods may be labelled as Vegetarian or Vegan if the ZC is under 10%.
- Exemption: All food suppliers to UK Government offices must adhere instead to **EU** regulations. This is to aid the Government in understanding the EU competition.

New and exciting opportunities for the Dead are exemplified by these recent job advertisements:

Quality Assurance Technician (Z)

Location: Basingstoke.

We are a growing, family run, biscuit manufacturer based in the heart of Basingstoke. We're taking full advantage of the latest trade deals and modernised UK food import standards. We have significant external security, watchtowers and a nearby military base making us ideally placed to exploit our zombie workforce.

The Role: As a QAT(Z) you will follow instructions from one or more living Quality Assurance Supervisors. You will inspect the quality of all incoming raw ingredients to the factory. You will ingest samples on a daily basis and 'report' on any pathogenic or mutagenic properties. Do not worry, you are not required to perform any decision making – your Supervisor will observe you at all times and identify occasions when our raw ingredients do not meet our strict safety standards.

The Person:
- You will be dead. No chancers. All applicants must undergo medical tests for confirmation.
- Knowledge/interest in consuming substances of unknown origin and non-traditional food ingredients.
- Willingness to work Monday-Sunday

and undertake a small amount of travel (on your eventual dismissal the nearest zombie disposal facility is 50 miles away).

Benefits:
- Job Security – we take your security very seriously. You will be monitored 24/7 while on your shift and we include free physical restraints as part of your uniform.
- Complementary meals – in addition to the ingredients you will consume on shift we offer complementary meals twice a day. Zombies can help themselves to **unlimited** biscuits from our award-winning canine and feline product ranges!

Wine Maker (Z)

Location: Kent.

You'll find the Tyramine Vineyard just a short 1hr train ride from the historic and beautiful town of Royal Tunbridge Wells. Tyramine

Wine is known throughout the UK as the finest available without incurring significant import tariffs. Our wine-making embraces pre-industrialised methods where all maceration is performed manually. Manual maceration is great for the environment and makes us the largest Dead employer in Kent.

The Role: You will be one of our 6000+ zombie Wine Makers. You will begin your day in one of our many 30k gallon vats where grapes start their journey to become one of Tyramine's boutique wines. Your job consists of one thing only – stomping on grapes to release their juices and begin fermentation. You will stomp every minute of every hour; nothing could be simpler.

The Person:
- 2 (two) working legs + feet are preferred. Single legged zombies will be considered if accompanied by a British Winemakers Hopping Qualification (BWHQ Level 4).
- Do you have unexplained gaseous emissions from your skin? If so, you may be deployed to our sparkling wine facility.

Benefits:
- Promotion Opportunities – on joining

Tyramine you will be working on our Red wine production line. After 3 months you will be considered for promotion to our White wine production line. Note: our White wine requires a much lower level of zombie contamination – you will be expected to lose **at most** 5% of your body mass in a single 72-hour shift (0.01% for wine exported to the EU).

Healthcare

In the year 2018 only 968 nurses and midwives from the EEA joined the Nursing and Midwifery Council's register, whereas 2015 saw over 10,000 joining. A fall in the value of the pound over the period also meant that any money earned in the UK was worth less in their home country.

Even before the twin impacts of Brexit and the rise of the Dead, across the NHS there was a shortage of almost 100,000 staff. Estimates of between 5% and 10% of the Health workforce had come from other EU countries. These pressures combined resulted in a shortage of 250,000 staff needed in the UK healthcare market by 2025.

Swindon Medical College ran two years of zombie nursing courses (2023/24 and 2024/25) to determine the ability of the Dead to deliver frontline medical services. The results were disappointing, the students displaying minimal levels of empathy towards patients and an unhealthy preoccupation with craniotomy, neuroendoscopy and other types of brain surgery – all topics that were notably absent from their Nursing Fundamentals syllabus.

With even the most basic nursing ruled out, the

Department for Health and Social Care brought in consultancy firm Smith, Henrick & Henrick, to adopt a blue-sky thinking out of the box approach without boiling the ocean. The result was a republishing of the NHS Long Term Plan appended with "v2.0" and accompanied by a new logo described by Smith, Henrick & Henrick as revealing *"the different sides of healthcare, the precision of our shared purpose, the depth of our heritage and the value proposition brought by our zombie workers"* – the new logo was a small red square. The only other change to the Long-Term Plan was a single sentence prefixed to the start of the document that read *"It is the recommendation of this report that the Dead should be employed to increase action on prevention"*.

So how are our zombie colleagues improving the health of the British public? Let's look at each of the key prevention commitments in turn:

Smoking – using the Melnyk Method over 10,000 addicts have given up smoking. The success of the Melnyk Method lies in its simplicity. To get started, the smoker collects all their cigarettes, lighters and matches and puts them in the possession of their zombie carer. The carer keeps the full supply secure and quickly learns the unique smell of tobacco. Some simple conditioning training ensures that the carer will sympathetically attack their patient if they attempt to access their supply or if indeed, they detect the scent of illicit smoking.

Alcohol – the Melnyk Method can equally be used to reduce or eliminate alcohol consumption. Care must be taken however if patients are tackling both smoking and alcohol at the same time. Several tragic house fires have been attributed to the combination of lighters, matches and alcohol strapped to a zombie with poor coordination and very little sense of self-preservation.

Obesity – nearly two thirds of adults in the UK are overweight or obese. Obesity is linked with type 2 diabetes, high blood pressure, high cholesterol and increased risk of many diseases and cancers. Key to combating obesity is addressing poor diet and improving physical activity. It is with the latter that the Dead are making Britain fit again. Launched in 2026 the "Cartouche to 5K" running plan takes absolute beginners, pairs them with a zombie personal trainer and gets them running 5K in just two weeks. It was developed by renowned scientist Dr. Kevin Walterhouse who sums it up nicely: *"Quite simply it is incredibly motivating to have an unmasked zombie tethered behind you on your morning run. We've only had positive feedback.*

Literally no one has told us that they failed to keep up the pace. Remarkable!"

Air Pollution – on this commitment the government has adopted a synergistic approach combining a modernisation of air quality targets with zombie "pollutant inhalers". EU Directive 2008/50/EC aka Cleaner Air For Europe (CAFE), set out legally binding limits for air pollutants that impact public health. Now liberated from EU law the UK has set new democratic levels that meet the needs of our ever-popular manufacturing industry. Where hotspots of dangerous particulate matter and nitrogen dioxide do occur, we now see the rapid deployment of Zombie Inhaler Teams. These specially trained teams are able to consume otherwise fatal levels of emissions, clearing an area the size of a football pitch in under three hours.

Childcare & Primary Education

Ever since the unforeseeable tragedies in Chorley (2020), Blackpool (2021), Preston (2021), Morecambe (2022) and Accrington (2022), the Dead are not permitted to work unsupervised in childcare **anywhere** in the UK.

When the Lancashire Education Board (LEB) decided in 2019 to allow zombies to work in the Early Years/Primary Education sector few could have predicted the niggling issues this would have presented. The LEB operated a business-friendly range of policies, energised by the post-Brexit devolution of powers from Westminster. St. Jospeh's Primary School in Morecambe employed four Dead staff who delighted hundreds of pupils in expressive dance lessons. Similarly, Little Bunnies Nursery in Blackpool delivered a 1:2 child to carer ratio and record low £5 per day fee by hiring a majority zombie workforce.

As we now know, dark clouds were coming and problems were first hinted at following the horrific massacre at the Jungle Party Soft Play (Chorley, 2020), when the 24 zombie Soft Play Assistants suddenly embarked on a blood thirsty rampage in a largely self-contained environment. The government were quick to set up an independent public enquiry into the incident led by Lord Beancroft (owner of the UK's largest private educational trust). Sadly, the Beancroft report was repeatedly delayed as the scope of the report was progressively increased with each incident. By the time the report was completed in 2024 it covered events in no fewer than 53 institutions ranging from minor bites to "significant infant losses". The surprising summary of the report noted *"As the number of incidents has increased and more reliable data has been collected, it has become clear that there are some concerns with the Dead working in very close proximity to infants. Many of the young people affected by the attacks lacked the necessary training, or perhaps common-sense, to effectively deal with their new supervisors and guardians. While sympathetic to the needs of the education and childcare employers, it is the recommendation of this report that the use of the Dead in these sectors should be paused until further research can be performed."*

What followed was countless years of empty teaching posts and sky-high nursery fees. The good news is that following the Beancroft Act (officially the Post-Mortem Childcare Employment Act, 2028), the Dead are once again able to seek employment in the childcare/education market.

Ordinary citizens should understand some of the key provisions in the Beancroft Act:

- Prior to undergoing supervision by zombie employees all minors must successfully complete Key Stage 1 + 2 courses in the four essential skills of reading body language, close quarters combat, trauma first-aid and hostage survival. While these courses are very serious, they are designed to be, at their core, a fun and entertaining experience. Children will enjoy a mix of classroom-based learning and highly realistic role play scenarios. Free counselling is available for all students.

- Once under supervision by zombie employees all minors must have appropriate Personal Protective Equipment (PPE) – remember that under ZombiEU legislation the Dead are exempt from PPE so responsibility lies with parents & guardians to ensure that their children are properly protected. Typical school uniforms include long sleeve/long leg with a Kevlar weave, sometimes with metal or ceramic "trauma plates" for additional protection.

- All affected institutions – schools, nurseries, holiday clubs and playschemes – must have a nominated Protection Officer (PO) on site at all times. The PO is liable for responding to out of character behaviour from the normally well-behaved Dead employees. If for example, an unruly child torments and provokes a working zombie into an unpredictable and ferocious attack, it is the duty of the PO to subdue the child's behaviour and limit their access to the Dead employee. As a last resort the PO is permitted to use *reasonable force* to control the zombie – for which they are armed with their iconic bamboo truncheons.

Points-Based Immigration

The Treaty of Rome created the European Economic Community (EEC) in 1957 and established the freedom of movement for workers in the EEC area, later the EU. In the decades that followed intelligent opinion shifted to the principle of operating as a sovereign nation with a high-quality points-based immigration system (PBIS).

After frequent promises of the benefits of moving to a PBIS after Brexit, it came as something of a surprise to many that the UK had been operating a PBIS since 2010 administered by the UK Border Agency. This proved particularly useful when the government had to rapidly implement a new system to cope with deceased immigration.

Post Zombie-Apocalypse the UK government rushed through legislation to establish an

Australian Style PBIS for the Dead. The minor flaws present in the legislation are outweighed by the tremendous economic boost the imported zombie workforce has brought to the country.

Tier 1 (Investor)

The investor subcategory is for those zombies who have left a significant inheritance that can be invested in the UK. In 2026 the investment thresholds were increased to £5M and £20M. An invested inheritance of £5M grants a zombie indefinite leave to remain after 5 years, the £20M threshold shortens this to just 2 years.

Tier 2 (Skilled Zombies)

This tier covers skilled zombies with a job offer from a UK-based employer. There are several categories under Tier 2 including Security, Childcare, Actors, Hazardous Environments and General.

Tier 3 (All Other)

This Tier applies to all zombies seeking entry to the UK who do not qualify under Tiers 1 or 2.

Points Scoring

Entry under Tiers 2 and 3 requires applicants to be awarded a suitable number of points. Tier 2 requires 50 points while Tier 3 requires 100.

Here's some of the points awarded as written in the Act of Parliament:

Attribute	Max Points
Aged under 35 at time of zombification	30
Killed fewer than 3 humans	20
Education or training in Australia	10
Graded less than 5 on the Marfleet Decomposition Scale	25
Working limbs	30
Consumes Vegemite and Chicken Parmigiana	40
Understands Cricket	15
Tolerate temperatures up to 50 Celsius	20

Soon after publication of the UK's zombie Points Based Immigration System questions were raised over the irregular allocation scheme. It was quickly realised that the requirement for an **"Australian Style"** system was misinterpreted by the cross-party committee formulating the system. Still, with a busy legislative agenda the choice was made to make the system work regardless of the inherent problems.

The impact of our Australian Style PBIS has been wide-ranging with some unexpected new business opportunities:

- Over 300 million jars of Vegemite are now imported to the UK annually. Due to increased post-Brexit import tariffs this generates nearly £650 million in tax revenue for the UK, more than any other single product.

- Twelve colleges now offer the "Cricket for Zombies" NVQ. This unusual course attempts to teach zombies the basics of cricket in just 32 weeks. A shorter "reminder" course is available to zombies who attended public school.

- Australian born zombies have found themselves automatically qualifying for settled status in the UK. In response to the rapid reduction in their Dead workforce the Australian government established a rival "British Style" PBIS. This has seen 2 million Dead emigrating from the UK to Australia seeking employment. The UK now exports 40,000 metric tonnes of Marmite annually, 98% of which is destined for Australia.

Food

Of most concern to consumers immediately after the referendum result was the potential impact from Brexit on the UK's food supply. While some suggested we would all pull together with our inherent Blitz spirit others politely highlighted that this was the country where citizens called the police when their favourite fried chicken restaurant ran out of chicken. Ultimately there was little to worry about – the Brexit deal was struck and implemented with the EU by August 2016 and the following year the rising Dead became the hot topic on most people's social media feeds.

The UK chickpea supply
Chickpeas have been farmed by humans for thousands of years and are the key ingredient in an extensive and diverse range of dishes including Moroccan houmous, red pepper houmous, reduced-fat houmous, sweet chilli houmous and caramelised onion houmous.

Between June 2016 and August 2016, the average UK household each stockpiled approximately 400 tins of chickpeas in preparation for Brexit. This proved an unnecessary precaution and resulted in warnings of an impending "chickpea mountain" if the public did not consume the chickpeas responsibly. You will have all received the Government's "Chickpea Cookbook 2017" and delighted in month after month of the now British-favourite dishes such as chickpea curry, chickpea smoothies, chickpea on houmous, chickpea a la pois chiche, chickpea n' chips and deep-fried chickpeas.

Fishing
Back when Britain was a member of the EU it was signed up to the controversial Common Fisheries Policy. This agreement allowed member states to fish freely in the territorial waters of other states. The UK's territorial waters remain some of the most fertile in the world so it is only right that, with control fully taken back, we alone fish our waters to the max.

The amount of fish landed by UK vessels has been steadily rising from 400,000 tonnes in 2022 to 1,200,000 tonnes in 2028 (the last year figures are available). The UK diet has similarly changed in the last decade to make use of the vast herring and mackerel stocks available in UK waters and therefore evading import duties. The great British pub menu is now replete with classics including Mackerel Vin Blanc, Mackerel Provencal and Swedish-Style Pickled Herring.

How has the UK achieved this three-fold increase in fishing in just ten years? The Department for Fisheries, Sport and the Arts successfully implemented an ambitious 3-point plan:

1. **Bait** – under EU law (regulation EC 1069/2009) fishing bait was limited to animal by-products from aquatic animals, aquatic invertebrates and larvae. Recognising this absurdly limiting regulation the UK's Fisherman's Freedom Act 2024 permits the use of zombie by-products as fishing bait. If you are engaged in freshwater or sea fishing (as a hobby or commercially) you can now use zombie parts as bait. Remember that you must still adhere to ZombiEU regulations so any zombie bait must have fallen naturally from the decomposing host.

2. **Demersal Fishing** – the demersal zone at the bottom of seas and lakes is home to popular species such as plaice, sole and cod. The practice of bottom trawling is used worldwide to catch large numbers of demersal fish with often significant environment impacts – sadly we see many EU nations continuing to destroy our fragile planet. The UK now leads the world in environmentally friendly, hand-

picked demersal fishing largely due to the pioneering work at the Grimsby Zombie Fishing College. Katherine Edmonds, the college chancellor explains: *"Fresh zombies make excellent fishermen. They are able, with appropriate weighted boots, to explore the seabed and hand-pick hundreds of fish per day. Here at Grimsby ZFC we train the Dead to recognise high-value fish species by touch (it's dark down there). There is a balancing act to our process; Once the zombie fishermen reach 5 on the Marfleet decomposition scale their effectiveness drastically diminishes. Rather than retire, many of those zombies freely and enthusiastically continue their studies through our new Trampolining and Bait Production course."*

3. **Security** – UK flagged fishing vessels are expected to support the Navy and enhance the security of UK territorial waters. To this end most fishing crews carry at least one (though typically four) Zombie Security Torpedoes (ZSTs). The latest British made Mark III ZSTs use a pair of 800cc Jet-Ski engines to power an adult zombie through the water at speeds up to 120mph. Under UK maritime law fishing captains may, if they feel threatened, launch a ZST at any suspicious vessels

they encounter. It is worth noting that all owners of the older Mark II models should return them to the distributer **immediately** for a free upgrade. A manufacturing fault in the Mark II resulted in an imbalance of engines (400cc port, 800cc starboard) earning them the nickname of the "boomerang torpedo" and the tragic loss of 129 British fishing crews.

Microbiological Criteria

Is your food safe to eat? How many days until the hazardous bacterial content makes it unsafe for human consumption? Do I need to test for Salmonella, Campylobacter or Enterobacteriaceae? It is these basic questions that the intelligent British food-consumer has been able to answer themselves for centuries. And yet in recent years the answers were dictated by EU regulation EC 2073/2005 (microbiological criteria for foodstuffs). New guidance from the Department for Public Health and Food Waste Elimination is as follows:

- Smell your food. The human nose is 25 times more sensitive to E. coli than the noses of whales. Use your natural abilities!
- The 5-day rule (formally the 5-second rule): British homeowners proudly maintain some of the cleanest carpets and

floors in the world. Laboratory tests revealed that a packet of crisps left lying on an ordinary British kitchen floor for 5 days remains perfectly safe to eat. Government guidance states that any foodstuffs (including meats, fish, fruit and vegetables) dropped on the floor are safe to eat until the 5-day point.

- Should you be particularly concerned about an item of food why not invite your Dead relatives over for dinner? Zombies make great test subjects for all your mealtimes. Be sure to serve your Dead guests first, observe their reaction (if any) to the meal and safely proceed to consume the tasty dinner without worrying.
- If you find maggots on your food ask yourself - did they fall onto the food from a leaking ceiling or a passing bird? It is not safe, or financially prudent, to assume that the maggots grew from eggs on the food itself. Brush the maggots off and do your bit to eliminate food waste. If in doubt try storing the food on the floor for 5 days.

Frequently Asked Questions

This final section of the guide is dedicated to answering the most interesting questions posed by readers of the First, Second and Third Editions of this book. The author would like to take this opportunity to thank the tens of readers who took the time to send in their excellent questions and to thank the millions of readers who thought about asking a question but were probably too busy.

It is also an opportunity to once again ask Marjorie Baker (Portsmouth) to please stop asking the same disturbing question. The author will refrain from reproducing the question here, but for Marjorie the answer remains the same "Yes, it's almost certainly illegal. Significant collateral damage is likely. No, the author doesn't want to hold it for you."

On with the questions:

Q: How does Brexit and the Dead affect the UK participation in Eurovision?

A: As you may have noticed the UK has continued to participate in Eurovision long after Brexit. Eligibility to compete depends entirely on membership of the European Broadcasting Union which is unrelated to the EU. Indeed, next year's contest will be hosted in Japan (the previous winners) and the UK will once again compete, hoping to escape our run of concurrent 12 nil-points including lasts years entry *"You should love us more, we're British damn it."* Eurovision rules changed in 2026 to permit zombie backing-singers & dancers and changed again in 2028 to allow zombies to both write and perform the song. Who could forget the all-Dead French entry from 2029 *"je ne peux plus marcher, mais je t'aime"*, or from the same year the rousing German anthem of unity *"Ich bin ein Zombie, du bist ein Zombie, wir sind alle Zombies."*

Q: What is an FAQ?

A: Interestingly this is the most frequently asked question the author has received – 78 readers have all posed this same tricky question to which as answer remains stubbornly elusive. Some cursory internet searching failed to provide a definition despite the term being used on millions of websites. There doesn't appear to be a zombie apocalypse or Brexit link to the term "FAQ" so the author assumes its usage predates both of these events, indeed there are indications that is has its origins as far back as the 17th century. Further research is needed.

Q: Is climate change still an issue?

A: The science remains inconclusive with formally dependable scientists unable to agree on a unanimous position. We can take comfort in the latest research from the International Coalition of Fossil Fuel Manufacturers (ICFFM) that reports a massive theoretical reduction in greenhouse gas emissions since 2020. The research assumes a twin-effect from Brexit and the rising Dead. Regarding Brexit, the ICFFM concludes that the 98% reduction in imports and exports to and from the UK has contributed to a 0.06% collapse in emissions globally from shipping goods. Similarly, the zombie population exhibit their tremendous green credentials by virtue of not breathing. Every Living human meanwhile exhales 2 tons of carbon dioxide every year. Our zombie friends have helped us to reduce our CO_2 emissions by a startling 3.8 billion tons – that's 4 times more than the entire air travel industry! The time for doubt is over, we've solved the climate crisis.

Q: Can I easily out run a fresh zombie?

A: Probably not, despite what you may have read in other less well researched guides. The top speed of a fresh zombie is **21 mph**. Unless you are an elite athlete you are unlikely to be able to reach or maintain that speed.

Q: Who can countersign a Zombie Visa?

A: There are much stricter standards for zombie visas than we are used to for passports and Living visas. The list of professions able to countersign a zombie visa is therefore much shorter and limited to government approved "sovereign occupations". If you need a zombie visa countersigning you must seek out one of these professionals: trade negotiators, politicians (plus their family, friends, business associates and passing acquaintances), journalists (from Category A approved press outlets) and chiropodists.

Q: Why did the zombie sponsorship scheme get closed down?

The Zombie Sponsorship Scheme (ZOSPOS) ran from 2026 to 2030, raised over £700 million in charitable donations and provided over 100,000 zombies in need with support, accommodation, medical care and employment assistance. Following a low-key media campaign, the savvy British public soon recognised this generosity had cost the Treasury £175 million in Gift-Aid contributions. A petition soon followed gathering well over 2,000 signatures leading to the scheme being quietly mothballed.

Q: Did Brexit cause the zombie apocalypse?

A: No. The zombie apocalypse can be loosely but unquestionably traced directly back to the flu outbreak of 1918. Certain "experts" have attempted to show causality between Brexit and zombies with zero success. None. There is no legally proven link between the reduced standards for biohazard storage and the coincidental outbreak of mH1N1.

Q: What is the Marfleet Scale?

A: The Marfleet Scale is the British Standard to measure the extent of a zombie's decomposition. It ranges from 1M (fresh), through 5M (loss of up to 2 limbs) up to a maximum of 10M (essentially a puddle). All UK zombie legislation uses the Marfleet Scale e.g. employment law & sick leave for zombies. By comparison the EU simply repurposed ISO 936:1988 (meat testing standards).

Printed in Great Britain
by Amazon

48832038R00059